Little Children

CHILDREN AND JESUS

Retold by *Anne de Graaf*
Illustrated by *José Pérez Montero*

BROADMAN
& HOLMAN
PUBLISHERS

CHILDREN AND JESUS

Published in 1999 by Broadman & Holman Publishers,
Nashville, Tennessee

Text copyright © 1999 Anne de Graaf
Illustration copyright © 1999 José Pérez Montero
Design by Ben Alex
Conceived, designed and produced by Scandinavia Publishing House
Printed in Hong Kong
ISBN 0-8054-2072-X

Dedicated to Pedro Pérez Rollán and to Elizabeth Cortright

6

This book is about being called and listening. This is something children are very good at. Who does the calling? Jesus. Who is being called? YOU!

7

One day, when Jesus was a little boy, Mary and Joseph lost him in a crowd. They called and called.

Where was Jesus? He was in the temple, teaching teachers about God.

What should you do when you hear someone you love calling your name? Can you whisper your own name very softly? That's how it sounds when Jesus calls you in your heart.

9

Many of Jesus' special promises
were about children. When he was
on earth he called people to him to
teach them how to show kindness
to children.

Name one kind thing someone did for you today.

Jesus promises to care for children in a special way. When children pray to God, he hears them.

Jesus watches over you all day and all night. His special helpers, or angels, watch over you too. How many angels do you think are in heaven?

Jesus never wants a child to be lost and afraid. He calls and calls and searches and searches, just like a shepherd searches for his lost lamb.

Find somewhere to hide now and have the person reading to you come find you. See how happy you both are!

There once was a mother from another country who begged Jesus to make her sick little girl better. Jesus listened as she called to him.

All people are different, some people do not live near us or look like us. Jesus loves everyone and wants us to love them too. He made the little girl well.

Jesus often calls to people who need him. At the end of a long day of teaching and healing, Jesus' closest friends said he should let everyone go home. "They're all so hungry."

Jesus called, "Who has some food?"
A little boy stepped forward. "I have
some fish and bread, sir. I will share,
but it's not much."

But Jesus shook his head.
There was more he wanted to teach.

All the people grew still. Jesus looked up. He called out to God and thanked his Father for the food. Then Jesus blessed the bread and broke it into many pieces.

Surprise! There was more bread and more fish. More than enough food for everyone! When Jesus blesses what you share, it makes a BIG difference.

Jesus liked to teach, especially children. Jesus teaches if we believe in him, we become his special followers.

Jesus knows children are very special. When he calls to them, they listen to what he says.

Jesus thanked his Father for the children. Often, children know and understand things that older and smarter people miss. He often called the children into his arms and blessed them.

Sometimes children can see things adults cannot. This is another reason children are so special. Name one thing special about YOU!

One day, Jesus was in the temple, and called for all the people to listen. Then he healed the sick and helped the blind to see. Everyone was happy except Jesus' enemies.

Are you happy when you see some-one being helped? Jesus taught that the really happy people are the ones who need God and lean on him every day.

Jesus' friends sometimes argued over who was the most important. "I'm the most important!" said one. "No, I am!" said another. Jesus pointed to a nearby child. He said, "Those who are like little children are the most important."

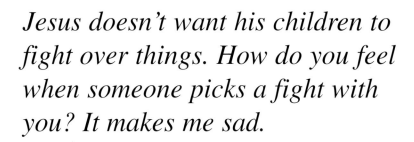

Jesus doesn't want his children to fight over things. How do you feel when someone picks a fight with you? It makes me sad.

34

Jesus said, "Whoever welcomes a little child, welcomes me. And whoever welcomes me, welcomes God my Father."

See how important children are! Who will you call tomorrow to welcome to your home?

Jesus' friends once told some children, "Go away. Leave Jesus alone!" But Jesus told them, "No! Let the children come to me."

I know my name, what's yours? Shout it! Jesus knows your name, too. Think how he might sound when he calls you.

37

A NOTE TO THE big PEOPLE:

The *Little Children's Bible Books* may be your child's first introduction to the Bible, God's Word. These stories about *Children and Jesus* are about the special times Jesus spent with children when he walked the earth. This is a DO book. Point things out and ask your child to find, seek, say, and discover.

Before you read these stories, pray that your child's little heart would be touched by the love of God. These stories are about planting seeds, having vision, learning right from wrong, and choosing to believe. Pray together after you read this. There's no better way for big people to learn from little people.

A little something fun is said in italics by the narrating animal to make the story come alive. In this DO book, wave, wink, hop, roar, or do any of the other things the stories suggest so this can become a fun time of growing closer.

38